PRAISE FOR THE POETRY OF JOHN KOETHE

"As funny and fresh as it is tragic and undeceived, *Falling Water* ranks with Wallace Stevens's *Auroras of Autumn* as one of the profoundest meditations on existence ever formulated by an American poet."

—John Ashbery on *Falling Water*

"To describe with uncompromising candor the inner life of a man adrift in the waning of the twentieth century is one thing, but to do it without a shred of self-pity is another. Koethe, with a riveting and limpid intelligence, manages to do both."   —Mark Strand on *Falling Water*

"'This secret life / Whose language is the melancholy sound the heart makes / Beating against its cage': this is John Koethe's subject in his beautifully constructed and deeply moving new book of poems—lyrics of the dark and painfully honest inward gaze."

—Marjorie Perloff on *The Constructor*

"Starting from Stevens ("Sunday Evening!") and ending . . . never ending, Koethe's voice is raised in an indefatigably eloquent phraseology of inspection (the nostalgias, the anticipations, the fatigues)."

—Richard Howard on *The Constructor*

"The voice is sober, meditative, rising now and then to the austerely lyrical. The intelligence is lucid, unsparing, yet infused with love of the world, the only world there is."   —J. M. Coetzee on *North Point North*

"*North Point North* is an excellent summation of this very fine poet's work, highlighting those qualities of clarity, grace, and precision that have characterized his writing throughout his career. It would be hard to imagine many better books of poetry."

—*Milwaukee Journal Sentinel* on *North Point North*

About the Author

JOHN KOETHE is Distinguished Professor of Philosophy at the University of Wisconsin–Milwaukee, and he is the first Poet Laureate of Milwaukee. His collection *North Point North* was a finalist for the Los Angeles Times Book Prize. His collection *Falling Water* won the Kingsley Tufts Award. In 2005 John Koethe was a Fellow of the American Academy in Berlin.

ALSO BY JOHN KOETHE

POETRY

Blue Vents

Domes

The Late Wisconsin Spring

Falling Water

The Constructor

North Point North: New and Selected Poems

PHILOSOPHY

The Continuity of Wittgenstein's Thought

Scepticism, Knowledge, and Forms of Reasoning

ESSAYS

Poetry at One Remove

Sally's
Hair

poems

JOHN KOETHE

HARPER ● PERENNIAL

NEW YORK ● LONDON ● TORONTO ● SYDNEY

HARPER ● PERENNIAL

A hardcover edition of this book was published in 2006 by HarperCollins Publishers.

HarperCollins books may be purchased for educational, business, or sales promotional use. For information please write: Special Markets Department, HarperCollins Publishers, 10 East 53rd Street, New York, NY 10022.

FIRST HARPER PERENNIAL EDITION PUBLISHED 2007.

Designed by Jeannette Jacobs

The Library of Congress has catalogued the hardcover edition as follows:
    Koethe, John.
        Sally's hair : poems / John Koethe.—1st ed.
           p.   cm.
        ISBN-10: 0-06-078943-3
        ISBN-13: 978-0-06-078943-5
        1. Title.
        PS3561.O35S25 2006
        811'.54—dc22   2005046123

ISBN: 978-0-06-117627-2 (pbk.)
ISBN-10: 0-06-117627-3 (pbk.)

07 08 09 10 11   ❖/RRD   10 9 8 7 6 5 4 3 2 1

ACKNOWLEDGMENTS

The poems in this book first appeared
in the following magazines:

American Poetry Review: "16A:," "Proust"

Antioch Review: "In the Dark," "Poetry and the War"

Boston Review: "Hamlet"

Fulcrum: "The Gift Undone," "When There Was Time"

Gulf Coast: "The Disquieting Muse"

Kenyon Review: "Sally's Hair," "The Middle of Experience,"
"The Unlasting," "This Morning"

Notre Dame Review: "The Maquiladoras"

Octopus: "Continuity and the Counting Numbers"

parlorgames: "Götternachmittag"

Poetry: "Collected Poems," "Piranesi's Keyhole,"
"The Perfect Life"

Southwest Review: "Aubade"

The Canary: "Adelaide"

TriQuarterly: "21.1," "A Tulip Tree," "Eros and the Everyday," "Midtown," "To an Audience"

Some of these poems were included in the pamphlet *Sally's Hair* (Sydney: Vagabond Press, 2004).

"Adelaide," "Eros and the Everyday," "*Hamlet*," "The Unlasting," "Piranesi's Keyhole," and "This Morning" were reprinted on the Web site *Poetry Daily*.

"To an Audience," was reprinted in *Best American Poetry 2004*, Lyn Hejinian and David Lehman, eds. (New York: Scribner, 2004).

"Sally's Hair," was reprinted in *Best American Poetry 2006*, Billy Collins and David Lehman, eds. (New York: Scribner, 2006).

To Diane

CONTENTS

The Perfect Life

I have a perfect life. It isn't much,
But it's enough for me. It keeps me alive
And happy in a vague way: no disappointments
On the near horizon, no pangs of doubt;
Looking forward in anticipation, looking back
In satisfaction at the conclusion of each day.
I heed the promptings of my inner voice,
And what I hear is comforting, full of reassurance
For my own powers and innate superiority—the fake
Security of someone in the grip of a delusion,
In denial, climbing ever taller towers
Like a tiny tyrant looking on his little kingdom
With a secret smile, while all the while

Time lies in wait. And what feels ample now
Turns colorless and cold, and what seems beautiful

And strong becomes an object of indifference
Reaching out to no one, as later middle age
Turns old, and the strength is gone.
Right now the moments yield to me sweet
Feelings of contentment, but the human
Dies, and what I take for granted bears a name
To be forgotten soon, as the things I know
Turn into unfamiliar faces
In a strange room, leaving merely
A blank space, like a hole left in the wake
Of a perfect life, which closes over.

Eros and the Everyday

as when emotion too far exceeds its cause
ELIZABETH BISHOP

A field of unreflecting things
Time is passing by: inert,
Anonymous beyond recall, the deflected
Objects of a self-regarding gaze
Untouched by the anxieties of proximity or love.
I tried to find those passions in the sky,
In moments when the heart surveys itself
As if from above, and wonders at the
Sight of something so particular and small.
A day brings language and a hint of what it means,
Of some presence waiting in the wings
Beyond the stage, beyond the words that
Gathered in the night and stayed
And through whose grace I find, if not quite
What I wanted, then everything else:

The contentment of each morning's
Exercise in freedom, freedom like a wall
Enclosing my heart; the disjunctive thoughts
Gesturing at some half-imagined whole;
A continuity that on the surface feels like love.

What is this thing that feels at once so nebulous
And so complete, living from day to day
Unmindful of itself, oblivious of the future
And the past, hovering like a judgment
Above the future, the present, and the past,
Floating in the distance like the eyes of love?
Call it "experience"—that term of art
For time in an inhuman world
Indifferent to desire, the history
Of one who one day wandered off from home
Along a road that led from here to here:
These sidewalks and these houses, city streets
And suburbs and a highway flowing west
Through fields and quiet streams, uncharted
Trails descending to a farmhouse in a glen and
Nothing in my heart or in the sky above my heart.
And then from somewhere in that wilderness inside
I hear the murmur of a low, transforming tone
That fills the field of sight with feeling,
And that makes of blind experience a kind of love.

Let me stay there for a while, while evening
Gathers in the sky and daylight lingers on the hills.

There's something in the air, something I can't quite see,
Hiding behind this stock of images, this language
Culled from all the poems I've ever loved.
I don't believe a word they say, a word *I* say,
But it isn't really a matter of belief:
As ordinary things make up the world,
So life is purchased with the common coin of feeling,
Feelings deferred, that flower for a day
And then retreat into the language. And later,
When the hours they'd filled are summoned by a name,
It's as if they'd never been, as if that tangible
Release could never come to me again.
I came here for the view, and what is there to see?
The place is still a place in progress
And the days have the feeling of fiction, of pages
Blank with anticipation, biding their time,
And ever approaching the chapter in the story
Where it ends, and my heart is waiting.

The Middle of Experience

My fear and my ambition: that my life
Remain the same, unchanging in its versions,
Constant as the street I lived on where the
Houses bode their dreams beneath a California sky.
That place is at the heart of what I mean,
Yet when I ask myself when I'll return to it again
The question seems more urgent than the answer,
Coming, as it does, at the end of something—poetry?—
Composed of endless summer afternoons
I can't imagine anymore, and fictions that created
Fictions of their own, yet somehow told
A story of a life indefinite as life,
Happening as it passes, leaving in its wake
An ease of mind and clarity of heart
Like a beautiful day. You want to bask in it,
Which is where you start: the middle of experience,

In a particular place, at a certain age—
In my case in Milwaukee, fifty-six,
My father dead just short of ninety-two,
The house in San Diego sold.

That house was *unbelievable:*
The fliers, when the stuff inside was sold,
Described it as a "decorator's house"—
The rooms like jewel boxes or the interior
Of a Fabergé egg, designed to conceal the facts
Of being old, the boredom and the pain,
The minor pleasures of anticipation or a lovely day,
The chair in which he sat for hours following the light,
Kept company by his catalogs and cat.
After my mother died I wrote a poem
About the presence of a vast, inhuman world
Hidden behind our lives, as if a thing too close to see
Might finally be made visible in death.
Yet this time nothing seemed revealed: the
Neighbors kept their counsel while the realtors came and went
Beneath the flat blue sky I'd known since childhood;
The hospice overlooking Mission Valley
Kept its secret from the warm December day;
The new year promised a "renewal of experience,"
An idea I've never understood.

I wonder if that thought has less to do
With feeling than a sense of place, a sense that
Comes to you the way ideas usually do—

Between breaths, or in the shower,
Or on a walk around the neighborhood
On a cool day in early spring. That can't be right:
This sense is of an *absence* of a place, a freedom
From constraint, the freedom of a part of me
Inhabiting this poem, and a part I left at home.
I like the image of a lime-green sky
Above a house two thousand miles away,
But distance doesn't matter, and the color—well,
It pleases me, that's all. The lights were on,
The keys were in the kitchen as I closed the door
On what once had been my life, that it might start again—
As though each day were a departure
And forgetting were the real renewal of experience,
Making the commonplace seem strange
And taking me to a place I'd been
So many times before, for the first time.

This Morning

To see things as they are is hard,
But leaving them alone is harder:
Snow in patches in the yard,
The vacuum in the sky, and in the soul
The movements of temptation and refusal.
I felt a day break. Nothing happened.
The windows gave upon a street
Where cars drove by as usual to the faint,
Unearthly measures of a music
Whose evasions struggled to conceal a
Disappointment all the deeper that the
Hope was for a thing I knew to be unreal.
I can't do it yet. Perhaps no one can do it yet.
The unconstructed gaze is still a fiction
Of the heart, a hope that hides
The boring truth of life within the limits

Of the real, a life whose only heaven
Is the surface of a slowly turning globe.
Yet still I want to think I woke one day to—
To *what*? The crystal trees, an earthly silence
And the white, unbroken snow of a first morning?

In the Dark

Call it a consciousness
Constrained by no relation
To another, surviving
In an imagination

Where nothing is ever lost,
But merely diminished,
Making out of it a
Life that remains unfinished,

Always on the verge,
Limping from day to day.
The possibilities
One summer takes away

The next restores in turn,
As each year supplants
Whatever came before it.
There are gifts time grants:

The specious serenity
Of age that hides the fear
Of an anonymous
Future. An unshed tear

For what never happened
Or that happens now
Too late. No disappointments,
Just amazement at how

Much there is to see
And how little it all matters—
Words; some poems like rags
Lying about in tatters;

Idiotic questions
That fascinated once
And now seem frivolous;
The fact of sentience.

It isn't what one wants
But what one has to choose—
Those who want everything
Inevitably lose

Everything they had.
What are the real measures
Of a complete life?
The imaginary pleasures

Of a world like an
Imaginary park?
The salt taste and strength
Of a body in the dark?

It seems so obvious,
But the trick is letting go.
What makes a simple choice
So hard? I don't know.

Continuity and the Counting Numbers

One is differentiable; the other depends
On things that you can see and set out in a line.
One measures change, the other intervals.
One lets you trace out what you've been or are
Or might yet become; the other is a row of tombstones
That you pass along the course of an existence
Broken into years, the units of a formula
In a single unknown waiting for you at the end.

The Disquieting Muse

Funny how it seems inconsequential
In retrospect, and then a tune begins
That flies you to the moon and then the stars.
The next one mouths the same sweet promises
Time pretends to keep, that matter now
That life is here again, yet seems so far away.
And for a while it seems suspended
As on the brink of some magnificent abyss,
An atmosphere of artifice that cloaks the tones
Of the indifferent truth that lies behind the seeming.

They all got into their cars and drove away.
I walked back to the house where maybe I was born
(Where *was* I born?), a fiction to myself.
The subject tries to spread itself across the sky,
Leaving it to puzzle at the trees, the debris on the ground,

The wilted leaves that are the real harbingers of spring.
Consumed by dread, a guy waits clueless at his desk
As the muse (or so she *says*) fingers herself
While the fragments gather in the corners, listening
To the song in the sky, anxious to begin.

A Tulip Tree

It's all here, present and unaccounted for,
With nothing to explain besides the
Wonder and the heightened sense of self
Engendered by these natural enormities
Without a voice or anything to say:
A tulip tree, the brute fact of a lake,
The morning light reflected from a placid
Surface hiding an interior unease
Occasioned by their beauty, taking it all in
Without understanding, for it makes no sense.
What distinguishes constructed beauty
From a beauty that's already there?
Kant tried to answer that—a unity
Without a purpose, nature's intricate
Indifference to our needs—
But I've never understood it very well.

Look at the light that fills the leaves,

The flowers on the tulip tree, the lake that

Wears its cloak of a translucent summer blue.

I see them as I read, and yet there's nothing

On the page but signs extracted from a vacuum by an act of will.

The same forms sprung from nature and imposed;

The same shapes brought to life by light and air

Created by some words I chose here in the darkness of my

        room—

Why should the myth of naturalness hold sway, the cult of

Authenticity prevail when accident and artifice

Can both be equally untrue to what we feel and mean?

Life has no form, not while it passes, and what settles into

Place in retrospect is just a story left around from childhood.

It's all there is, and incomplete. But in that lack

I find a thing I've looked for all my life:

A complement to life, a monument to unreality

That makes a world of difference. Beside each day

There lies another day, responding to the will

Of whoever creates it. Call it a place of freedom,

But its beauty is the beauty of the question

Of a different life, indistinguishable from this one

And transforming it, that it might

Answer in its way, and be understood.

Piranesi's Keyhole

Here it is then: no constraints,
A future that extends as far as I can see,
As far as I can stand it. Follow me
Along the path of my ambition, through a maze of days
That make up what I want to call my life. Come with me
Of an evening, when the day is at its clearest,
Or a morning when its promise still feels immanent and new.
Be patient. Sit motionless before a page
That holds the image of a face, its questions
Answered by the May sky's deepest blue;
Or put it down to age, or to the way time feels as it passes.
I kept these thoughts contained for over fifty years,
Concealed in what I thought of as a home,
One thousands of miles away, which as its spell broke
Pressed into my consciousness a sense of being
Utterly alone, and in that loneliness completely free,

Untamed by time's constraints or by a world

Of mere seeming, a place of pseudomemories

In which the past is ashes and tomorrow is a wilderness

Of drugs and dreams and trees like clouds and clouds like trees—

A place of air, where everything occurs by choice

In the space of a few minutes; where songs go on forever

And transport me to the threshold of an antiworld

Of no more substance than the words that give it voice, unfolding

At the stately pace of a recitative. Bear with me now,

For if you ask how much of this I literally believe,

I don't know what to say—not much, I guess.

I know though that I love the way it passes, as it changes

Boredom to a smile and makes the air seem sweeter while it lasts.

Is it so terrible to try to keep the world at bay,

To treat it as an exercise in make-believe? Some say so,

But to me what matters is the going back and forth

Between two different minds, both incomplete, the liberty to disappear

Into the freedom of a daydream or the freedom of the street.

And when I question what that anonymity might mean

I see a nothingness of sky above the dome of a cathedral,

Or the ruins of some villa overrun with weeds;

I see through Piranesi's Keyhole the hallucination of St. Peter's

Floating in a space and time beyond a corridor of trees,

Or hear the sound of voices I can't recognize in what used to be my home.

There is a place existing only in the mind, or minds,

Approachable through memory or art, an aesthetic counterpart

Of that imaginary world Kant called the Realm of Ends,

That answers only to the laws of its creation. It begins,

If it begins anywhere, in childhood—in a story out of Poe,
Or in a church, or in a private moment glowing with the sense,
Not so much of another life, as that this one is wanting—
Which is also where it ends. We're grown-ups now,
Long past the need for what the stories told us, for a *somewhere else*
Beyond the tangible realities of daily life, beyond the veil.
I know. Yet it isn't in the end a matter of belief, but of an impulse
Rooted in experience, too indeterminate to be a thought,
That says you have to go there though you know it isn't true

—Which is where I started: with a future at my fingertips,
Permissions granted, free to chart the terms of an existence
"Loos'd of limits and imaginary lines." And for a time
I went along with it, enchanted by its promises of a liberty
Of thought and purpose, purpose flowing into action
In a synthesis of feeling and idea, mind and heart. And in a way
Its promises came true, though not the way I'd wanted:
No imaginary lines impede me, nothing intervenes
Between my life as I conceive it and its presence on the page,
Unburdened by the facts of getting older. You see,
I knew the place beyond the keyhole was a figment of my mind,
Albeit one whose fiction was created in my heart;
But what I didn't realize was that the mind containing it
Was unreal too, the specter of a speech delivered from a stage.
And just as one is a creation not to be believed,
So too the soul, for what it glimpses through the aperture of art
Is Berkeley's world, existing simply as perceived,
A haven for the eye that seeks it or the vagrant self
That looks around and tries to call it home,

That celebrates the freedom of its Realm of One,

A freedom purchased at the price of unreality. Who cares

What I believe or don't believe? This voice that speaks to you

Isn't the voice of a person, but the subject of a reverie.

I wish—it started with a wish—at this late hour

I could find a different way of talking, one embodying the life

Of something like a person in an ordinary world;

That I could find a way to place that life in context,

Showing it both as it is and as it wants to be—

But that will have to wait, for having come full circle

And remaining of two minds, I take my leave.

II

The Unlasting

I

Like a vain man practicing a vain art
Born out of failure—not the grand failure
Of the Will or the Imagination,

But on a more human scale: *what happened?*
What happened to the incidental life
You try to make up, though it falls apart?

Each year I come again to where I am.
What happened to that place I meant to make,
That whole of which I meant to be a part,

A whole with space for other people too?
I don't know. The solace of a daily
Hall of mirrors and the nightly bedlam

Of my own dreams—they gradually dissolve
Into a pleasant day in early spring,
A water-color sky and leafless trees,

All waiting. What I want is what it gives,
Which ought to be enough for me for now—
My strategy is simply to resolve

To see it through, whatever it might bring,
And hope that something *other* should emerge,
That words that come to me along the way

Make up a document that chronicles
A solitary life, bounded by hope.
And so I offer you these rites of spring.

II

A certain life begins and ends with God,
Not as a tangible reality,
But in the abstract, as a nagging sense

Of something lacking, or of something else
Remaining to be said beyond the facts.
The world is all that is the case, complete

In itself, with nothing else beyond it.
Slowly, as it attempts to take it in,
The soul, confronting something so immense,

Is reduced to an insignificance
From which it rises once again in thought
Until at last its triumph is concrete

—That's the delusion: of another way
Of living both within and through the world
That makes experience a sacrament

And intimates a vision of a life
Too vast for its surroundings, magnified
By the endless struggle to make it fit.

Wittgenstein again: "Running against the
Walls of our cage is perfectly hopeless."
But it stands as a living "document

Of a tendency in the human mind
Which I cannot help respecting deeply.
I would not for my life ridicule it."

III

Could *that* have been my life? It isn't now.
The truth is that I'm lackadaisical,
Content to let the moments come and go

Without a thought for what the years might bring
Or what comes afterwards. Like everyone,
I suppose, I daydream about music

And sex and food; my faults are common ones;
My virtues too. As for mortality
And eternity, all I really know

Is what I've read, which isn't very much.
Poetry helps, but usually conveys
The bare sense of life at its most basic.

I feel like someone waiting to begin
A story without a real ending,
Opening in the middle of the way

And going on from there, page by page
Throughout the night, until the sun comes up
And it's time to start all over again.

Beneath it all I feel the silent rage
Of the unspoken, what gets left unsaid
In the narrative of the everyday:

That here and now can be a prison too,
That of the man who tries to hide himself
Behind the transparent walls of his cage.

IV

I think that it's impossible to give
An explanation of experience
That captures how it feels and what it is

Sub specie aeternitatis, something
Seen from deep space, from just above the earth,
Or even from this city where I live

And where I find myself adrift and free,
Making my way along a busy street
In April, moving with the speed of song

Across a page, with visions of people
Coming as close to me as my own name,
But remaining oblivious of me.

Is there a measure of experience?
Some change that it effects, an altered sense
Of life that follows in its aftermath?

Or is there something it aspires to,
Some changeless ideal it contemplates,
To which it promises obedience?

I think it vanishes before our eyes,
Like something that had never even been.
The day begins in waiting, in the hope

That what I felt once I might feel again
—A fallacy completely obvious,
Yet one so difficult to realize.

V

And so I find myself inhabiting
A kind of no-man's-land between the thoughts
Of earth and heaven, living on the line

Between a once and future life, between
The passive and the possible, through words
That see through both of them and see them through.

I know they're both absurd. The question
Isn't of what to think or what to do,
But what to do without. The choice is mine,

I'd like to think, and whether to abjure
Those fantasies is simply up to me.
It's not that easy though. For if I knew

What lay beyond them or could take their place
In the mythologies I listen to
To tell me what to feel and how to see,

This fear of letting go might dissipate
Like this morning's fog, leaving me at peace
And reconciled to what I had become.

A picture held us captive: but my dream
Is to walk away from it, emerging
Into a space with room enough for me

And me alone. I want to lose myself
In what I've thought and felt and seen, and then
Avert my eyes and let that kingdom come.

VI

And then to my astonishment it did.
Time passed. I found myself remembering
A day in college, then another day,

All real days made up of accidents
And things and people that I'd really known,
And places where I literally had lived

And which had been as much a part of me
As this apartment now. For by assembling
All of them into a rambling story

Ranging over distant times and places,
I'd given them a being of their own,
A life that felt continuous with mine.

And suddenly the light that filled the trees
Came from a summer forty years ago.
An ordinary April day assumed

The effusive California colors
Of an autumn afternoon, when the sun
Has burned away the early morning haze.

Could that be what Proust meant? I think it is:
That time, which seems relentless in its slow
Approach to anonymity and death,

Is impotent against the will of art;
That nothing disappears; that once begun
Its epiphany goes on forever.

VII

He asks you to believe that a release
From the constraints of time, a quiet state
In which the present and the past seem merged,

Opens on a suffocating bedroom
Furnished with the past, with sempiternal
Moments laid up in a sanctuary

Outside of time, or better still, submerged
Beneath the currents of the everyday—
A transport ending in deliverance,

Like a journey down an estuary
Flowing at last into the open sea.
I don't believe it. Yesterday is fixed,

And yet its possibilities remain,
Its sense of feeling "absolutely safe,
Whatever happens," whether on the way

To the store, or sitting on a park bench
Looking at the cars, the clouds, that airplane
In a slow descent towards Mitchell Field.

And even in the middle of the day
This sense is of the presence of the past,
But in an immanent, more human form—

Not as a hidden heart that lies concealed
Beneath the skin of ordinary life,
But here in its moments, which come and go

VIII

And where this daydreaming finally ends—
Not in a quiet recess in the mind,
But on an afternoon that seems a vast

Cathedral brimming with an earthly light
That shows things as they are, and lets them go.
Why do we want to bring them back again?

What does it *mean,* "the presence of the past,"
If not a pang at how things disappear,
A love of the unlasting, brought to earth

By the pervasiveness of change? And when,
In a fleeting moment of distraction,
The light seems that of a distant morning

In New York, an afternoon in high school
In the shade of a bungalow, it's not
That they'd been waiting but that they were gone.

These things were good because they had to die.
They vanish, and the traces that they leave
Are part of nature too, a part of us

That wants to keep them as we wish they were.
I took the past for granted. I forgot
How much of it we fabricate, how much

Of my life is actually a story
Mixing what I want and what I believe
With some words that retell it from within.

IX

The first failure, from which the others flow,
Is to live entirely in a world
Of your own making, and to live alone.

Whatever else I started out to find,
What I've arrived at is a kind of place
—A temporary one—I never left,

That I can neither alter nor postpone.
But it's not going to last: like everything
Under the sun a poem has its day

Or year or years, and then—what? Time is theft,
But in the long run what it takes away
Comes back as something numinous and strange,

That simply having lived through seems enough.
I know the tone, and what it tries to say.
I know the measure of reality

Isn't what I say to myself, but what
Another person tries to say to me,
Who turns to me and smiles, and turns away.

There is an air of unreality
About this place, as though I looked at it
Through someone else's eyes. And what I see

Is nothing but an ordinary day
Transformed, unlike all those I've known before,
And so strange. And I think it's wonderful.

X

Let it get dark, and the inessential
Noises fade into the mild April night,
Leaving just the houses, a hill, some trees

And stretching out as far as you can see
A lake illuminated by the moon,
By the moon illusion. Low in the sky,

As though hanging just above the water,
It shines at the end of a path of light
Beginning at the shore and flowing east.

Ascending, it gets smaller, finally
Becoming, like a spell that breaks too soon,
A stone in the impersonal night sky.

When I was a boy my bedroom window
Looked out upon a range of soft brown hills.
Beyond them lay the desert and the East,

A country cloaked in a green I'd never
Seen until I took the bus to college
That brought me in the end to where I am—

An odd place, yet one I must have chosen
Long ago, like a promise time fulfills
In passing, that comes too late, that leaves me

Floating in the air between a fleeting
Glimpse of nothing and the common knowledge
That lay waiting for me beyond the hills.

III

A u b a d e

It's early, but I recognize this place.
I recognize the feeling, after an endless
Week of mornings in America, of returning
To the home one never really leaves,
Mired in its routines. I walk to what I try to
Tell myself is work, entering at the end of the day
The same room, like the man in *Dead of Night*—
The dinner, the DVD from Netflix,
The drink before I go to sleep and wake alone
In the dead of night like Philip Larkin
Groping through the dark at 4 a.m. to piss,
At home in the reality of growing old
Without ever growing up. I finally get up
An hour later, run, eat breakfast, read and write—
A man whose country is a state of mind,
A community of one preoccupied with time,

Leaving me with nothing much to do
But to write it off to experience—the experience
Of a rudimentary consciousness at 5 a.m.,
Aware of nothing but the drone
Of its own voice and a visual field
Composed of dogs and joggers in a park.

To an Audience

I knew the artifice would finally come to this:
> An earnestness embodied in a style
More suited to the podium than to the page,
> Half sight, half sound, an antipastoral
With which to while away a vagrant afternoon.
> The stage is set as for a play, with cotton
Clouds and cardboard trees beneath a foil moon
> That fails to illuminate the scene.
If you believed in me—if what I meant to say
> Resonated in your heart; if a tone
Held your breath and caught your feeling for the world;
> If my thoughts were thoughts that you alone had had—
The reality would be the same: the summer day
> Outside, indifferent to the other day
Tranquillity and time conspired to create.
> This is my arena—this is the stage

On which I mean to live, an isolate domain
          Bounded by silence, inwardly consumed by
Music whose relentless cadences resume
          The speculations of that secret self
For whom to even try to talk to you is death.
          These are the stanzas of a single story,
Spun from unconnected moods that ebb and flow
          Across the surface of the day, from words
Implicit in my breath and spoken to a mirror.
          I get up, retrieve the newspaper
And read myself into a stupor. Then I write.
          I know these habits are a ruse, the tricks I
Use to keep the world at bay, to keep alive
          The fiction of the soul as self-contained.
Yet even as I speak its character is shifting
          As the light shifts and I seem to hear
A disembodied murmur from the balcony
          In which I think I recognize my name.
What made me think that I could live apart from you?
          The folly of that thought now seems so clear,
With scenery and background drifting towards me as you
          Overrun this stage I said was mine.
My thoughts may try to hide themselves, to glow in private,
          Yet what animates the page is just the
Specter of a self existing in and through you
          As a forest finds itself in trees,
A city in its towers. This place is bathed in light,
          Revealing it for what it is, a crude
Pretence of thought, like children playing with some blocks,
          Unconscious and alive to one another.

Let my purpose hence be plenitude and patience
      In the hope that through their common grace
I might eventually attain that generous
      "Condition of complete simplicity"
That musing on the thought of you has let me see.
      I'm grateful to you then for all your questions
And objections—for indeed you *are* objections—
      And that is all, for now, I have to say.
Let us conclude though with some resolutions: to
      Abjure these fierce conundrums of the soul;
To quit this theater of dreams; to walk as one
      Into the light of ordinary day.

Adelaide

for Kevin Hart

It was a wonderful time, and we,
Its creators and subjects, were never more alive.
There were rumors in the bars and bookstores,
Reputations, giddy conversations
In the cabs, on the long walks home after the readings.
Some stood the test of time, some flourished
For a day, but all knew what the shouting was about
And who the heroes were. And then it was over—
Pessimists or optimists, we didn't *matter* anymore,
At least not in *that* way. There is this sense of place,
Though not of purpose, yet the place itself feels unfamiliar
As we rub our eyes and look around with but a hazy
Sense of what we stand for, who we are.
What *are* our mottos? Who is this *we*?

Meanwhile the gnome was at his spinning wheel,

Defying reason, defying even the defiance of reason,

Stranded in that dreamtime where the stream flows on forever

In cascading clauses sometimes spilling over on a page,

But mostly shadowing the darkness in the heart

Where the real poem begins, and ends.

What have *I* conceived? Some thin, bright clouds

Through which an airplane gradually descends

On the other side of the world? The crowds o'erflow the tents

In the February heat along the River Torrens

Where the tunes roll on all summer long,

Yet seem so local now, and too immediate to believe.

Why can't I just repeat the songs I learned in singing school?

But those seem futile, much too far removed

From what I feel here in the isolation of my room.

Come here to the window. Let me show you my street.

The Gift Undone

The land remained foreign, brooding beneath
A country whose illusions it sustained.
The land maintained the semblance of a place
Made wary of itself, and so unmade.
In Florida, in California,
The future seemed to whisper in the sky
Above the undone country—an assent
Withheld, a covenant unraveling
Like a dream of shady, tree-lined streets that
Lead inexorably into a maze
Of high walls and empty, sun-drenched sidewalks.
Its anthem still continued in the night
On the verge of sleep, the tip of a tongue,
As close as someone's name: anonymous,
Amnesiac, forgetful of the words
For what it was, for what it had become.

When There Was Time

Physics and—what?—existentialism?
Guitar heroes and singer-songwriters
And death? You were supposed to write poems
Breath by breath, movies were as serious

As novels, and tomorrow was the name
Of a different kind of life, a life
Beyond imagining, hiding in the
Darkness behind the adolescent sun.

The same sun rolled like clockwork through the sky,
Monitoring the road to who knew where,
That trailed off into the shrubbery.
And there was time to find that road again,

To follow its invisible design
And argument, preparing for a place
Of nuance, shadow, and complexity,
Where adolescence was supposed to end.

Who'd want to go there now? There's *always* time,
But when I think about the future now,
It's of a world already done, without
The promise or the threat of difference.

Coming out of a movie (*Best in Show*)
This afternoon, near the corner where the
Oriental Pharmacy used to be,
It seemed to me I'd lived there all my life:

That the theories were all formulated,
The songs all written and sung, and that time—
Not the time of the nostalgias but the
Time of history—had come to an end.

I know that this is age, and only age.
Why should the way time felt when one was young
Change how it feels today, with everything
So static, with the afternoon so still?

I want the darkness back, both in the sky
And here in my heart, that it might remain
Uncharted, still a stranger to itself,
Oblivious of what it was, and change.

The Maquiladoras

They oversimplify our lives,
These stories, stripping them of context and detail,
Recasting each one as a journey, moving from the country
To a factory on the border, from a rural home

To one that I'd imagined, to this place
That I inhabit, locked in the idea
Of a room, a home, a city street, the country
Where I live and I was nineteen once

And where I find myself a subject of two states,
Of two distinct domains: a private one
Of furniture and poetry, pottery and silent monologues
While shaving in a mirror, thinking through

A turn of phrase, the course of an emotion,
Tracing the trajectory of a thought
That takes me to the kingdom of a single mind
Where what I think and feel and say all seem the same.

We all live in the other one. On the news
Last night a woman in New Jersey
And a man in Pennsylvania read my mind. More dead
Filled up the screen as someone read their names

Instead of mine, which would have been the same.
More Wal-Marts in Chicago, on the sites
Of some abandoned factories, while the doors keep closing
On the maquiladoras in Tijuana and Juárez

Through which the money flows, and flows away. Who says
That life is change, and change is for the better?
It can look that way when looked at through the blinders
Of an individual life, one constantly embarking

On a journey of its own, of everyone's,
From adolescence through late middle age. Nineteen
Was nothing special and I wouldn't want it back,
Yet sometimes when I think about the years to come

I see almost as many as the ones since then.
I feel a vague and incoherent fear, a fear
Of waking from time's dream into an even stranger place,
As different from today as now is from nineteen,

Without a sense of where I am or where I'd been before—
Which is always here, in my imagination. When I ask myself
What home was really like the answer is sheer fiction,
As I picture to myself an endless summer

Sky above a Culver's or a Dairy Queen,
A school, the Hansen-Onion funeral home, the modest
Mansions on the quiet, shady streets
Of a small Wisconsin town time left unchanged.

Poetry and the War

The bombs bloom in the same green light
As 1991, the year before I started "Falling Water."
If I'd stayed over on that Monday afternoon
After Robert's memorial, and woken in that small hotel off
Wall Street with the towers falling, this war already begun—
But who knew that then? I try to write each spring,
Just attitudes at first, made up of what the season brings
Or what a year has changed. I try to rearrange them
Into what I am now, fooling with the words
The way some god might fashion individual lives
Into an intricate design apparent only to himself,
Traced out by a rocket's soft green glare.

God isn't dead, he's just a frat boy from the sixties
With a scared blank face and angry memories.
The proof is in the eyes, the repeated I's,

The monotone of grim indifference and disdain.
They speak the language of the restoration, of an idée fixe
Repeated everywhere, though no one says its name
And what the whole world knows is left unspoken
Like a silent poem, a measure of regret.
The king is in his countinghouse—an undisclosed location
Somewhere on the grid. Who did the calculations?
Who made up the words? Who cloaked this personality
In a rhetoric whose urge is simply to forget?

Some wars are fantasies. The bombs and deaths are real,
Yet behind them lies an argument played out in someone's mind.
Its movement is relentless and unplagued by doubts
Until one day you wake up to the fire in the sky, the change
That came about by increments and left a wilderness,
The wilderness of this century in which I'm finally going to die.
When I was young I wondered if I'd live to see it,
With its rational governments, its fantasies of transportation—
And now here it is. And I'm a part of it, without a say
In what it stands for or its all-consuming poem
Made up "of things ill done and done to others' harm,"
Done in my name. I feel ashamed and numb.

Götternachmittag

June is the indifferent month
The xebec sank at the end of *V*.
Think of a century as a park—
A beach at Normandy,

The Hall of Mirrors at Versailles,
An assassinated president—
Surrounded by a wilderness
Of banished incident.

Think of a person as a passage,
And personality as a choice
Between grandeur and the small,
Self-consuming voice

Ripe to be misinterpreted
As the voice of a mere satirist,
A depicter of surfaces.
The universe curls its fist,

Squeezing the soul into a ball,
A particle in a history
Written by either *them* or *it,*
As the case proves to be.

I passed into the afternoon
Of the gods, imprisoned forthwith
By the sweep of its narrative,
Paralyzed by the myth

Of those who'd had the privilege
To bear its cross, and then expire
Beneath its weight. How shall *I* live?
And how should I aspire?

Collected Poems

small war on the heels of small / war
ROBERT LOWELL

I think they may be adequate for now,
With summer finally in full swing
As imperceptibly the days begin to shrink.
Each spring I wonder what I'll find
When I return to them again—this year it was a war
That wasn't actually a war, a lie made visible—
And how blind intuitions might be built up into facts
That someone else might think to feel and read.
The signs are everywhere, implicit in the sky,
The trees, the houses on the street I walk along to work
(The walking *is* the work), when something that I see
Or half-remember gets repeated from inside,
Finds its measure, and in settling inward settles into place.
They're how I wander through a day, wondering at its
Spaciousness, finding in its anonymity

These traces of my name, in its impersonality
These ways to see myself—hearing in the syllables of the
Leaves the lyrics of a song; seeing in the clouds
A human face, another lie made visible.

Word by word and war by war—
What makes one possible sustains the other too:
The urge to change, the power to deceive,
To fabricate a version of the world
Not as it is, but as someone imagines it to be.
The aim is not to say what happened
But to forge a monument by force, deploying
All the subtlety and weapons of the will
And leaving something broken in its wake: the simple truth
As it appeared in school each day; the simple self
That wrote it down, before it all became a wilderness
Where what's still left of them still wander,
Looking for each other, through a mutual memory
Of something irrecoverable beneath these
Shifting sands of spoken and unspoken words.

I used to think there was a different way,
A less insistent one, accepting what it finds
Without revising it, without the specious clarity
And authority of art, and its pervasive
Atmosphere of will. But that turned out to be a style too,
A sweeter one perhaps, yet just as artificial in the end.
The point is general, not confined to art: to make
Is to destroy; to act is to replace what would have been

With something signed, that bears a name. When I was a boy
I thought a life just happened, or was there to find.
Wars were aberrations. Poems were another generation's.
I didn't realize you made it up, you made *them* up,
And that the self was not an object but an act,
A sequence of decisions bound together by a noun
But with the feel of a fact. I wonder where that leaves me—
Hanging on a whim, on what I write? I hope not.
What the urge to dominate the world, the place, the page
Eventually becomes is just a human figure
On a summer afternoon, smiling at what happens,
Anxious for the future and the slope of age.
I think I'm done for now. It remains to save the file,
Close the notebook, and let evening come.

IV

Midtown

Is it so ridiculous, at an age
Long past the age of the exceptional
And that city paved with gold and set for me,
To feel this sealed sense of self still
Breathing in the traffic of an April afternoon?
Sometimes I'd come in on the bus at noon
And walk around and have the perfect lunch I'd
Saved for and arranged, and walk around some more.
And I remember Scribner's and the galleries,
The brilliant stores and all those interchangeable
French restaurants with their Gallic names,
And once a recognition that that person
Staring from a mirror in the Metropolitan was me.
There's a Gap now where De Pinna used to be
And Chambertin closed years ago, and yet the sunlight
Falling on Fifth Avenue feels practically the same.
The clouds above St. Patrick's are the clouds from college.

A sphere of self set in a sea of average days
Bereft of purpose and of personality, a sea of passage
As though time were just a medium, a blankness
Summoned in tranquillity and then filled in.
It's not what fills it up but that it passes
And in passing re-creates the world, which remains
Unchanged. The crux is how you feel that world,
Constructed from the way you feel yourself,
Your friends, your feeling for the present and the past
And for a place where all these incomplete conceptions end.
For as I walked around today what struck me wasn't
What was different or was still the same—
Trump Tower vs. Tiffany—but just the inwardness
Of being there at all, a point of isolation on a
Former street of dreams that seemed demystified and small.
There really *was* a kingdom: it was in my head,
Beyond recall. There's nothing waiting for me now
But what was waiting for me then—a hotel room,
An evening with a friend, an ordinary place beyond a
Sealed consciousness impervious to change.
Grant me the heart to feel it and the sense to see.

21.1

What I remember are the cinders and the starter's gun,
The lunging forward from a crouch, the power of acceleration
And the lengthening strides, the sense of isolation
And exhilaration as you pulled away, the glory at the tape.

I never really got it back after I pulled my thigh my sophomore year.
I still won races, lettered and was captain of the team,
But instead of breaking free there was a feeling of constraint,
Of being pretty good, but basically second-rate—

Which Vernus Ragsdale definitely was not. When he was eligible
(He was ineligible a lot) no one in the city could come close—
No one in the country pretty much, for this was California. We had our
Meet with Lincoln early in the spring, and he was cleared to run.

I was running the 220 (which I seldom ran) and in the outside lane,
With Ragsdale in lane one. *The stretch, the set, the gun—*
And suddenly the speed came flowing back as I was flying through the turn
And all alone before I hit the tape with no one else in sight.

Friends said he looked as though he'd seen a ghost (a fleet white one).
The atmosphere of puzzlement and disbelief gave way to
Chaos and delirium when they announced the national record time
Of 21.1 and I stood stunned and silent in a short-lived daze—

Short-lived because the explanation rapidly emerged:
They'd put us in the quarter-mile staggers by mistake, to be made up
Around two turns, not one. I'd had a huge head start on
Everyone, on Ragsdale on the inside most of all. By the meet's end

Lincoln was so far ahead they didn't even bother to rerun the race,
And so we ran the relay, lost, and everyone went home—
Leaving me wistful and amused and brooding on the memory
Of my moment in what was now a slowly setting sun.

There's a story that I read my freshman year in college
Called "The Eighty Yard Run," by Irwin Shaw. It's about a football player
Who makes a perfect run one afternoon and feels a heightened sense of
Possibility and life: the warmth of flannel on his skin, the three cold
      drinks of water,

The first kiss of the woman who is going to be his wife. All lies before him,
Only he never measures up: gradually at first, and then more steeply,
It's a long decline from there, until he finds himself years later on that
Football field again, a traveling salesman selling cut-rate suits.

I'm not immune to sentimental cautionary tales: the opening door
That turns out to have long been shut; the promissory moment,
Savored at the time, with which the present only pales by comparison,
That tinctures what comes later with regret. I'm safe from that—

Track wasn't everything, but even minor triumphs
Take on mythical proportions in our lives. Yet since *my* heightened moment
Was a bogus one, I can't look back on it with disappointment
At the way my life has gone since then. Perhaps all public victories

Are in some sense undeserved, constructed out of luck
Or friends or how you happened to feel that day. But mine took off its mask
Almost as soon as it was over, long before it had the chance
To seem to settle into fact. I'm human though: sometimes I like to

Fantasize that it had all been true, or had been *taken* to be true—
The first of an unbroken string of triumphs stretching through to college,
Real life, and right down to today. I ran that race in 1962,
The year *The Man Who Shot Liberty Valance* was released,

A film about a man whose whole career was built upon a lie.
James Stewart thinks he killed—and everyone *believes* he killed—
Lee Marvin, the eponymous bad guy, although he never actually killed
        anyone at all:
John Wayne had shadowed him and fired the fatal shot,

Yet governor, senator, ambassador, and senator again
All followed on his reputation. He tries at last to set the record straight
—The movie's mostly one long flashback of what happened—
But the editor to whom he tells the real story throws away his notes:

"When the legend becomes fact," he orders, "print the legend,"
As the music soars and draws the veil upon the myth of the Old West.
Print the legend: I'd like to think that's what my story was,
Since for a moment everyone believed that it was true—

But then it wasn't anymore. Yet it's my pleasure to pretend
It could have been: when Willis Bouchey at the end affirms the fairy tale
With "Nothing's too good for the man who shot Liberty Valance,"
I hear in my imagination "who beat Vernus Ragsdale."

Sally's Hair

It's like living in a light bulb, with the leaves
Like filaments and the sky a shell of thin, transparent glass
Enclosing the late heaven of a summer day, a canopy
Of incandescent blue above the dappled sunlight golden on the grass.

I took the train back from Poughkeepsie to New York
And in the Port Authority, there at the Suburban Transit window,
She asked, "Is this the bus to Princeton?"—which it was.
"Do you know Geoffrey Love?" I said I did. She had the blondest hair,

Which fell across her shoulders, and a dress of almost phosphorescent
        blue.
She liked Ayn Rand. We went down to the Village for a drink,
Where I contrived to miss the last bus to New Jersey, and at 3 a.m. we
Walked around and found a cheap hotel I hadn't enough money for

And fooled around on its dilapidated couch. An early morning bus
(She'd come to see her brother), dinner plans and missed connections
And a message on his door about the Jersey shore. Next day
A summer dormitory room, my roommates gone: "Are you," she asked,

"A hedonist?" I guessed so. Then she had to catch her plane.
Sally—Sally Roche. She called that night from Florida,
And then I never heard from her again. I wonder where she is now,
Who she is now. That was thirty-seven years ago

And I'm too old to be surprised again. The days are open,
Life conceals no depths, no mysteries, the sky is everywhere,
The leaves are all ablaze with light, the blond light
Of a summer afternoon that made me think again of Sally's hair.

Proust

I don't remember how it started. In high school
I'd devoured "modern fiction"—Dostoevsky,
Joyce and Woolf, Fitzgerald, Faulkner, Hemingway
And Lewis (oops!)—but still no poetry. Why don't you
Read some Thomas Hardy? asked my English teacher.
Yet I persevered, and by the end of my third year in college
Reached the mountain waiting at the end. And thus
Began the summer of *Swann's Way, Within a Budding Grove,*
The Guermantes Way and half of *Cities of the Plain.*
I'd read them in my bedroom, on our patio in San Diego
Where my progress was the progress of a cloud
Across the endlessly receding skies above Combray.
The sentences, as you can see, proceeded at their pace,
The pace of life: I broke up with my girlfriend;
Poetry took some poems of mine; my summer job
Was cleaning floors in local schools; a letter from New York
Arrived to tell me Frank O'Hara (whom I'd met at

Dinner just three months before) was dead.

The pages turned: Odette, Gilberte, the Jockey Club

Assumed their places like the place-names on the rail line.

I was young. I tried to find my story written in the years

To come, but everything I found was something that I'd read,

Whose *raison d'être* was the imperative of reading on—

And so I left it all to chance, as summer ended

With the pollination dance of Charlus and Jupien.

Fall came, my final college year. I set his books aside

But found a surrogate, George Painter's marvelous biography

That focused on the same world through a different lens.

One night I let a Vox Box of French chamber music—Debussy,

Ravel, Fauré and Frank—play on and on throughout the night

As in the darkness of my dormitory room I dreamed about

That soundless room at 44 rue Hamelin. Then winter came,

And spring, and then commencement brought an end

To my "bright college years" and I went back to California,

Only to resume his endless monographs on Albertine and jealousy,

The Captive and *The Sweet Cheat Gone.* Life channeled art:

I fell in love and wrote my first long poem. Somehow I'd stumbled

Into graduate school, and soon the time had come for me to leave.

I read *The Past Recaptured* on the plane and on a bench in Harvard Yard

And on a Greyhound to New York to ship my things and visit John.

I told him I was nearly done. "This must be a tender moment,"

He replied. "Do you want to be alone?" I said I didn't,

So we went downstairs where I could meet "Old Stanley" Kunitz

(Old!—he's ninety-nine now; this was almost forty years ago)

At a party at the Cavallon's. The book ends with a party. Russell Baker,

When he'd finished, wrote a column in the *Times* that gave away the ending:

"There's this big party and everybody has gotten a lot older,"
Which about sums it up. Upstairs at John's I finally
Gained the final words—"so widely separated from one another
In Time."—reread them once or twice, and closed the book.

It changes you. You're a different person by the end,
If only since it takes so long to read. I used to tell myself
I'd read it one more time before I died, but long ago
I realized I won't. And so the boxed three volume set
I got how many years ago? sits on the shelf, a mute reproach.
Where did I find the energy, the time? A new translation
Of *Swann's Way* came out last year. I think I'll take it to Berlin—
I'm surely up to *that,* I'd like to think. Sometimes I take the old one down
And read the coda, where the narrator, now writing in the present,
Wakes at dawn and goes out to the park. The gym is closed
For renovations, so I've started getting up at 5 a.m. and running in Lake Park,
Milwaukee's own Bois de Boulogne, but on a smaller scale. "Marcel"
Is horrified by what he sees, by how it differs from the world that he recalls
—The hats, the clothes, the motorcars, the ripples on the real lake—
And yet what strikes me is how innocent it seems: the mist upon the golf course
And the white moon hanging in a pale sky still rosy in the east.
There's no one there. The world is waiting. Time feels like a structure
Waiting to be filled with scenes from the generic lives
We all lead, interchangeable, yet every one a story to itself
Whose truth lies in its style, the passage of that life
From childhood to here, complete with names and places
Fleshing out a novel's worth of days. No matter how detailed,
They disappear, and nothing can convey the simple truth
Of what each one was like, that sense of something now as
Indeterminate and fugitive, alas, as the years.

16A:

The apartment on Francis Avenue
We lived in for three years in graduate school
In the nicest—or maybe second nicest—part of Cambridge,
On the third floor of Joe and Annie's house

Just up the street from the Divinity School.
John Kenneth Galbraith lived next door;
Julia Child's Kitchen was across a backyard fence
I'd hang around trying to look hungry,

And emulating her we rented a meat locker at Savanor's,
Where I'd stop to pick up a pot roast or a steak
Before coming home to Jeepers waiting for me in the window.
Everything happened then, in two or three years

That seemed a lifetime at the time:
The War and SDS and music; the confusion in the streets
And Nixon; poetry and art and science, philosophy and immunology,
The dinners at Bill and Willy's loft in Soho—

Yet what still stays with me is the summer of 1973,
The summer before we moved to Milwaukee, with my dissertation done
And time to kill, suspended on the brink of real life.
I would read the first draft of "Self-Portrait"

John had let me copy, and *Gravity's Rainbow,*
And every afternoon I'd ride my bike to Bob's house
Where I'd watch the hearings on TV. And on a Saturday in June,
With the living room awash in the late yellow light

That filtered through the western dormer window,
We watched, just out of curiosity, this horse I'd read about
—And what I knew about the Sport of Kings was nil—
Turn what till then had been an ordinary day

Into one as permanent as anything in sports or art or life,
As Secretariat came flying through the turn with the announcer crying
"He's all *alone*—he's moving like a *tremendous machine,*"
And Susan shouting "Look at that horse! Look at that horse!"

The summer sort of dribbled away. We took a last trip to New York,
John and Rebecca stopped over on their way to somewhere,
James and Lisa too, whom I hadn't seen in years,
And then we packed our stuff and took the cat and drove away.

Nixon hung on for a while, and then—but that's history,
Real history, not this private kind that monitors the unimportant
For what changes, for what doesn't change. Here I am,
Living in Milwaukee twenty-nine years later.

Susan lives about a mile away, and just last Saturday
The latest wonder horse, War Emblem, stumbled in the Belmont Stakes.
What *makes* a life, if not the places and the things that make it up?
I know that *I* exist, but what about that place we lived? Is it still real?

—Of course it is. It just gets harder to see
As time goes by, but it's still all there. Last month in Rome
The first thing Lisa said was that I looked just like myself, but with
          white hair.
And there it is: look at the tiny strawberries and the

Flowers blooming in the garden of the house next door.
Look at John Dean, still testifying on that little screen, and Rogers,
Who died in May, still talking in our small blue dining room.
Look at Savanor's, the unkempt lawn, the mailbox by the back porch,

Jeepers waiting for me in the window. Look at that horse!

Hamlet

. . . a divinity that shapes our ends.

It was math and physics all the way,
The subjects of the life that I'd designed
In high school, that carried me away,
A callow California youth with Eastern dreams,
From home. The thought of something abstract
And aloof, penetrating to the heart of the unknown
And consigning everything else to the realm of unreality—
I didn't believe it then and don't believe it now,
Yet something in the fantasy felt so complete,
So like the lyrics of a song that spoke to me alone,
I bought it. How quaint that vision seems now
And mundane the truth: instead of paradox and mystery
And heroic flights of speculation that came true,
You had to start with classical mechanics and a lab;
Instead of number theory and the satisfactions
Of the private proof, a class of prodigies manqué

Made jokes in mathematics that I didn't get.

And there were problems with the style,

The attitudes, the clothes, for this was 1963,

The future waiting in the wings and practically on stage—

The Beatles and Bob Dylan and Ali, né Cassius Clay,

Who from the distance of today look like clichés of history,

But at the time seemed more like strangers in the

Opening pages of a story I was learning how to write.

The new year brought Ed Sullivan and track,

But what with winter and the little indoor track

My times were never close to what I'd run in high school.

I started hanging out across the hall—they seemed, I guess,

More "Eastern" than my roommates, closer to the picture of myself

That called me in the first place: Norwich, Vermont,

The Main Line and St. George's, and (I guess it figured)

A prospective civil engineer. And then there was New York:

I'd been in once or twice, though not for dinner,

So when James suggested Richard Burton's *Hamlet*

At the Lunt-Fontanne I fell right in. We went to dinner

At a place on Forty-sixth Street called Del Pezzo,

Up some steps and with bay windows and a chandelier.

We ordered saltimbocca and drank Soave Bolla

As I listened, Ripley-like, to recollections of three-hour

Lunches at a restaurant on a beach somewhere near Rome.

And then the lights went down, and when at last

The ghost had vanished, Burton strode upon the stage.

It was, I think, the first "bare" *Hamlet*—Hamlet

In a turtleneck, the rest in street clothes, virtually no scenery—

Leaving nothing but the structure of the play, and voices,

Burton's resonant and strong yet trembling on the brink of
Breaking, as for hours, from the first *I know not seems* until
The rest is silence, he compelled the stage. And then,
The bodies everywhere, the theater went black and we went
Somewhere for a drink and took the last bus home—

For by then I'd come to think of it as home.
By next fall everything had changed. My roommates
Were the former guys across the hall, sans engineer.
In San Diego Mr. Weisbrod from the science fair
Was appalled, as math and physics disappeared,
Supplanted by philosophy. A letter from the track coach
Lay unanswered by an ashtray, and I took a course
From Carlos Baker, Hemingway's biographer, in which I
First read modern poetry—*The Waste Land,* Moore, *The Cantos,*
Frost and Yeats—and dreamed that I might do that too.
I wish I knew what happened. Was the change
The outward resolution of some inner struggle
Going on since childhood, or just a symptom of the times?
So much of what we're pleased to call our lives
Is random, yet we take them at face value,
Linking up the dots. Feeling out of it one evening,
Staring at our Trenton junk store chandelier,
I started a pastiche of Frost ("In the mists of the fall…")
And even tried to write a play about a deadly clock
Styled on Edward Albee's now (alas) forgotten *Tiny Alice,*
The object of another Broadway interlude, this time a matinee.
Hamlet was forgotten. Pound and Eliot gave way
To Charles Olson and the dogmas of projective verse,

To Robert Duncan and the egotistical sublime,
And finally to "the Poets of the New York School,"
Whose easy freedom and deflationary seriousness combined
To generate what seemed to me a tangible and abstract beauty
As meanwhile, in parallel, my picture of myself evolved
From California science whiz into impeccable habitué
Of a Fitzgerald fantasy. It became a kind of hobby:
Self-invention, the attempt to realize some juvenile ideal
I cringe to think of now, playing back and forth
Between the guise of the artiste and of the silly little snob,
A pose I like to think of as redeemed (just barely) by a
Certain underlying earnestness. Perhaps I'm being too harsh—
I was serious about the path I'd chosen, one I've
Followed now for forty years. What life worth living
Isn't shaky at the outset, given to exaggerations and false starts
Before it finds its way? Those ludicrous personae were
A passing phase, and by my senior year whatever they'd concealed
Had finally settled into second nature. I'd go on,
But let me leave it there for now. My life after college
(Cf. "16A:" and "Falling Water") more or less continued on the
Course I'd set there, mixing poetry and philosophy
In roughly equal parts, vocation and career. My days
Are all about the same: some language, thought and feeling
And the boredom of the nearly empty day, calling on my
Memory and imagination to compel the hours, from morning
Through the doldrums of the afternoon and into early
Evening, sitting here alone and staring at a page.

You're probably wondering what provoked all this.

For years I'd heard they'd filmed a performance of the play,

To be shown just once and then (supposedly) destroyed.

Browsing on the Web about a month ago I entered,

Out of curiosity, "Richard Burton's Hamlet" into Google.

Up it came, available from Amazon on DVD (apparently

Two copies had survived). I ordered it immediately,

Went out and bought a player (plus a new TV) and watched it

Friday evening, calling up the ghosts of forty years ago.

I'd misremembered one or two details—it was a V-neck,

Not a turtleneck, at least that night—but Burton was

As I'd remembered him, incredible, his powers at their peak,

Just after Antony and Arthur and before the roles

Of Beckett, Reverend Shannon, Alec Lemas, George;

Before the dissolution and decline and early death.

Some nights I feel haunted by the ghost of mathematics,

Wondering what killed it off. I think my life began to change

Just after that performance in New York. Could *that* have been the

Catalyst—a life of words created by a play about a character

Whose whole reality is words? It's nice to speculate,

And yet it's just too facile, for the truth was much more

Gradual and difficult to see, if there to see at all.

We like to think they're up to us, our lives, but by the time we

Glimpse the possibility of changing it's already happened,

Governed by, in Larkin's phrase, what something hidden from us chose

And which, for all we know, might just as well have been the stars.

That adolescent image of myself dissolved, to be replaced by—

By *what*? I doubt those pictures we create are ever true—

Isn't that the moral to be drawn from this most human of the plays?

It isn't merely the ability to choose, but agency itself—

The thought that we're in charge, and that tomorrow mirrors our

Designs—that lies in ruins on the stage. It isn't just the

Life of a particular young man, but something like the very

Image of the human that dissolves into a mindless anonymity,

Dick Diver disappearing at the end of *Tender Is the Night*

Into the little towns of upper New York State.

I know of course I'm overacting. Burton did it too,

Yet left a residue of truth, and watching him last Friday

I began to realize there'd been no real change,

But just a surface alteration. Sometimes I wonder if this

Isn't just my high-school vision in disguise, a naive

Fantasy of knowledge that survived instead as art—

Aloof, couched in the language of abstraction, flirting

Now and then with the unknown, pushing everything else aside.

This place that I've created has the weight and feel of home,

And yet there's nothing tangible to see. And so I

Bide my time, living in a poem whose backdrop

Is the wilderness of science, an impersonal universe

Where no one's waiting and our aspirations end.

Take up the bodies, for the rest is silence.

BOOKS BY JOHN KOETHE

FALLING WATER
Poems

ISBN 0-06-095257-1 (paperback)

"As funny and fresh as it is tragic and undeceived, *Falling Water* ranks with Wallace Stevens' *Auroras of Autumn* as one of the profoundest meditations on existence ever formulated by an American poet." —John Ashbery

THE CONSTRUCTOR
Poems

ISBN 0-06-095635-6 (paperback)

"*The Constructor* is a scrupulous, elegant account of the meditative intellect as an instrument continually registering the passage of time. Exquisitely modulated and brutally honest, these poems would be harrowing were they not so seductively beautiful." —George Bradley

NORTH POINT NORTH
New and Selected Poems

ISBN 0-06-093527-8 (paperback)

"John Koethe's meditative poems have a tranquility which is both enchanting and deceptive: once inside the maze of his mind, we enter more and more worlds. Or is it the other way around? Mind into the world mind: dreamy, absorbing, alarming, these are poems to lose and find oneself in." —Rachel Hadas

SALLY'S HAIR
Poems

ISBN 0-06-117627-3 (paperback)

"A highly readable book, appealing in its elusive and somewhat eerie blend of the personal and impersonal, and compelling in the rigor of its inquiry into the human condition." —*Boston Review*

"Passionate, lyrical poems of great energy and provocative ideas."
—*Entertainment Weekly*